Mud Makes M

Mud Makes Me Dance in the Spring

Charlotte Agell

Tilbury House, Publishers
Gardiner, Maine

To my family,
especially my mother Margareta

Tilbury House, Publishers
132 Water Street
Gardiner, ME 04345

First Printing

Library of Congress Cataloging-in-Publication Data
Agell, Charlotte.
    Mud makes me dance in the Spring / Charlotte Agell.
        p.   cm.
    Summary: A young girl spends a spring day outside doing various activities with her family and letting her imagination soar.
    ISBN 0-88448-112-3 : $7.95
    [1. Spring--Fiction. 2. Family life--Fiction. 3. Imagination--Fiction.] I. Title.
PZ7. A2665Mu 1994
[E]--dc20
                                                                                          93-33610
                                                                                               CIP
                                                                                                AC

Designed by Edith Allard and Charlotte Agell
Editing and production: Mark Melnicove, Lisa Reece, Devon Phillips, and Lisa Holbrook
Office and warehouse: Jolene and Andrea Collins

Imagesetting: High Resolution, Inc., Camden, Maine
Color separations: Graphic Color Service, Fairfield, Maine
Printing: Eusey Press, Leominster, Massachusetts
Binding: The Book Press, Brattleboro, Vermont

Mud

makes me dance
in the spring.

It's everywhere,
even under the swing.

I fly into the sky,
I can pump by myself
all the way to the moon.

When my mother
gives me a giant push,
I might even end up on Pluto.

My brother can't swing.
He is a new baby.

We have to take care of him.

He eats all the time.
Sometimes my mama and papa
can't even play with me.

So I hide in the quince bush.

Here is my secret room

with a hummingbird.

I sit very still
but it flies away.

Fly away! Fly away!
Visit me another day.

A man comes along.
He asks, "Who are you?"

"I am the princess of the flowers.
I have no mother and no father."

"We have always wanted a daughter,"
says my papa.

So I come out of the bush
and we hug.

It is time for my haircut
and a popsicle after it's done.

Snip — snip — snip
The wind takes my hair.

The popsicle is red,
I share it with my brother.

It tickles his lips.

I like to help in the garden.
Poking holes

and planting peas is fun.
My knees get wet.

Our neighbor is here.
He has come to harvest
our dandelion greens.

He loves to boil them
and eat them with butter!

Suddenly, a bird flies by
with a snip of my hair
in its beak.

"Maybe she will weave it
into her nest,"
says my papa.

I am the princess of the birds!

My brother lifts up his arms
and cheeps like a chickadee.

He is the prince of the birds.

Other books in this series by Charlotte Agell

I WEAR LONG GREEN HAIR IN THE SUMMER
WIND SPINS ME AROUND IN THE FALL
I SLIDE INTO THE WHITE OF WINTER

For more information write or call:
Tilbury House, Publishers
132 Water Street Gardiner, ME 04345
1-800-582-1899 Fax 207-582-8227